DATE DUE

MUSE
ADVE

Free pass in

No. D

Whenever you see a red seal in the book, there's a puzzle to solve. Take a look at the sheets of parchment in the envelope at the back of the book. The solutions are hidden underneath the seals. Put your finger on the seal and slowly count to ten, or rub your finger over the seal. When the seal is warm, it will become transparent and the answer will be revealed.

If you see a skull, that means you are wrong!

If you find a symbol, you have chosen the right seal.

Make a note of the seven correct symbols! You will need them later.

Have fun reading and puzzle-solving!

Thomas Brezina

MUSEUM OF ADVENTURES

Thomas Brezina

Who Can Open Michelangelo's Seven Seals?

Illustrated by Laurence Sartin

PRESTEL

The Secret Chamber

Sometimes feet seem to have a mind of their own. They take you somewhere you never intended to go, but when you get there you have an adventure beyond your wildest dreams. This is one of those days. Your feet carry you to the bottom of a flight of wide steps, leading up to a tall, imposing entrance with a green wooden door. The door is reinforced with thick metal bands and strong screws, as if to say, "No one can enter when I'm closed!"

A dog is barking behind the door. It sounds very excited.

You are standing in front of an old building, three stories high. Its domed roof towers majestically above your head. Stone dragons stretch out from the edge of the roof, solid and dignified, staring straight over the houses of the town.

The dog is still going mad. The barking seems to be echoing from a large room with a stone floor and bare walls. It sounds like a cross between a mastiff, a St. Bernard and a hellhound.

You hear a gentle *crunch* from above, like someone grinding their toe in gravel. There's a trickle of fine sand and then another *crunch.* The noise stops, only to start up again almost immediately.

Again you hear a slight CRUNCH.

What's going on up there on the roof?

5

SHOCK! CONFUSION!

It's not just your feet that are behaving strangely today. Your eyes must be playing tricks on you, too. There's no other explanation. One of the stone dragons on the roof seems to be leaning forward. Its wings are spread as if it's about to take off and its mouth is now wide open. You can see right into its dark gray gullet. That's impossible. The dragon's made of stone and it can't have moved. But it looked different before. Now you get the impression that it's about to swoop down and gobble you up.

Impossible! That couldn't happen!

You hear a husky voice next to you. *"Someone's found the chamber."* A woman is standing right beside you, staring up at the roof. Where did she come from? She's so slim, she looks as if she'd barely cast a shadow. The high collar of her shimmering turquoise cape is turned up and she reminds you of a frilled lizard. A cloud of perfume surrounds her. It's a sweet rose scent that almost takes your breath away. Slowly, she turns her head toward you. *"The secret chamber!"*

Two large black-rimmed eyes with shimmering jade green lids gaze straight at you.

"Someone must have broken Michelangelo's seven seals."

It sounds as if the woman is telling you a secret.

What does she know?

What on earth are Michelangelo's seven seals?

A long finger with a sharp pea green-polished nail points at the building.

"Disaster, there could be a massive disaster. The owner of the museum can prevent it—so long as he hasn't been in the secret chamber himself!"

The old lock of the green door clicks and rattles noisily. The door opens and a dog shoots out. The biggest thing about him is his bark. With wild leaps, he races down the steps and jumps up at you. He just reaches your chest.

He must have trodden in some paint. His two front paws are red and yellow and his back paws are green and lilac.

A man appears at the entrance to the building, almost filling the doorframe.

"Pablo, here! Quiet! Sit! Heel!" he orders. You expect Pablo to greet the mysterious woman next to you as well, but the spot where she was standing is now empty. And the stone dragon on the roof? It's crouched there again like an obedient gundog, its wings folded back and its nose in the air. The wind chases the clouds across the sky and they seem to form a big

?

7

Who Is Madusa?

Pablo breathes in, then sneezes violently.

He sniffs excitedly at the spot where the mysterious woman was standing just a few moments ago. His master trudges down the steps in his worn-out slippers, snapping the wide suspenders that hold his bulging corduroy pants up over his rounded stomach. The man gives you a brief smile and reaches for the dog's collar. Then he seems to smell the sweet rose scent too and his bushy eyebrows knit together like a gray brush.

He straightens up slowly and stares down the street.

"Madusa," he murmurs. Her name seems to stir up an unpleasant memory. He turns to you and asks, *"Did you see a woman? With a greenish face and fingernails?"*

Yes, that was her.

The man notices your glance, which keeps returning to the roof.

He takes a couple of steps back and looks up.

The dragon
looms stony
and immobile
against the sky

Pablo presses himself against your legs, growling warily. A rumbling

8

noise rises from his chest and bursts out of his mouth as an excited **bark**. He begins yapping again, loud enough to make a hellhound flee.

This time the *CRUNCHing* is as shrill and as harsh as a blow from a giant sword.

The stone dragon spreads its wings threateningly and a long, thin tongue flicks from its mouth like a whip. It looks aggressive and ferocious as it leans right out toward Pablo, howling and grunting.

With a loud yelp, Pablo hides behind you and peers anxiously between your legs.

You feel the man grip your arm. He drags you toward the entrance and gives Pablo a sharp command, which is hardly necessary.

Cowering, the dog dashes ahead of you.

The roof of the porch protects you from what happens next. Small chunks of masonry rain down onto the pavement. This dragon doesn't breathe fire like the monsters of legend; instead, it spits stone.

The chunks **break** into pieces when they hit the cobblestones, scattering **splinters** in every direction.

"Inside, quick!" The man pushes you through the door and slams it behind you. The bang echoes through the pillared entrance hall where you are now standing.

"Don't be afraid, I won't hurt you," he reassures you as he pulls a heavy wooden stool underneath a high, narrow window.

"My name's Tonatelli. I own this museum."

Panting, he heaves himself onto the stool, which groans under his weight.

Pablo puts his paws on a second stool, inviting you to sit down like his master. He also wants you to lift him up so he can take a look out the window.

"Did Madusa say anything about the secret chamber and the seven seals?" Mr. Tonatelli wants to know.

Yes, she did.

The museum owner runs his hands over his round belly.

"I've heard of them, but it's a myth. It has to be a myth. How can it be real?"

The hail of stones outside the museum has stopped.

"You mustn't tell anyone what you have seen!" Mr. Tonatelli urges you. *"It might keep the visitors away and that's the last thing I need."*

Groaning, he gets up from the stool and stumbles off. Pablo struggles out of your arms to chase him, but after a couple of steps he stops and taps the floor with his front paws. He wants you to follow him.

Without once turning around, Mr. Tonatelli hurries down a long corridor, past some tall wooden doors that stand open, revealing large and small galleries.

The most famous picture in the world, the *Mona Lisa*, painted by Leonardo da Vinci, hangs in one gallery. She raises her hand and waves at you!

In another gallery, lined with red fabric, the faces of serious-looking men gaze out from golden frames. The second from the right is Michelangelo.

Although he may look like an overweight bear, Mr. Tonatelli shoots up the stairs to the second floor as quickly as a gazelle, then on to the third. He is heading for a circular room, lined with shelves from floor to ceiling. He turns around and around, searching for something, then claps his hands three times.

"Michelangelo," he calls. He sounds as if he's trying to attract an escaped parrot.

However, it's not a brightly colored bird that flutters down, but a book. And it doesn't exactly flutter, it tips forward and falls down from the top shelf.

Mr. Tonatelli catches it like a goalie would a soccer ball.

"Back! Keep out of the way!" he warns you and Pablo.

There is a sloping stand made of carved wood. He gently lays the book on it, takes a deep breath and opens the cover. The cramped room is immediately filled with the sound of tools striking rock. Tiny chips of white marble spray out from the book. As if rising from the deep, something appears from the wavy, yellowing pages.

"Keep this to yourself," Mr. Tonatelli demands.

What appears out of the center of the book looks like an egg, only much bigger—like a dinosaur egg. It's transparent, and filled with a swirling, bluish mist.

"This museum was founded by my great-grandfather. He wanted to create a museum full of marvels and adventures. He collected amazing and mysterious things from around the world, including this library." Mr. Tonatelli examines the egg-shaped mist impatiently and repeats insistently, *"Michelangelo!"*

The egg bursts and the mist disperses in all directions.

Who's that? Who's standing there?

As Mr. Tonatelli turns the pages, he says to you, *"So far as
Mr. Buonarroti was concerned, an artist was worth less than a
cobbler. But Michelangelo had his heart set on becoming a sculptor."*
Michelangelo Buonarroti—that was Michelangelo's full name, but
today we just know him as Michelangelo.
Mr. Tonatelli flips through the pages, as if this were just an ordinary
book. He opens it at a new page, and at first, mist wafts out as before,
but then figures appear.

Young Michelangelo immediately puts his chisel into the mouth of the statue. A couple of taps with a wooden mallet and a dark hole has appeared in the faun's mouth, just where a tooth used to be.

A pale blue mist rises from the paper again and envelops the young Michelangelo and Lorenzo de Medici, until they have completely disappeared.

Mr. Tonatelli snorts with frustration. Tufts of hair sprout from his wide nostrils. Quickly, he carries on leafing through the book, murmuring, *"Seal, seal, seal. I've read something about it somewhere."*

The page he stops at is blank apart from the heading.

HIS SEAL

There's nothing else on the yellowish paper, which is speckled with dark, glinting spots of mildew. It's not mist that wafts from the book this time, but a cloud of fine white dust. Tiny crystals swirl weightlessly in the light of the lamp, which hangs from the ceiling like a glassy green droplet. Two men appear out of the dust like genies from a bottle.

That Michelangelo looks just like a baker—only it's marble dust instead of flour he's covered in from head to toe. His back is coated in stone chips and his house is full of marble slivers and dust.

Painting is for women and weaklings!

Who is the man who compares Michelangelo to a baker? You can find the answer if you hold this page up to the light.

Michelangelo whisks the dust up with his hands, wafting it into the face of the other artist. The man fades like an old photo and disappears. The dust disperses, leaving a view of an enormous rock. Large slices have been cut from the mountain, as if from a giant cake. On the surface it is covered with earth, clay and gray stone, but the interior is dazzling white.

You, Pablo and Mr. Tonatelli blink and peer at it through half-closed eyes, so bright is the light reflecting from the white marble. Blocks as tall as a man are being rolled down to the valley on tree trunks. Piece by piece by piece. Michelangelo is standing in front of a tall block of marble with jagged sides. Around him are several broad-shouldered men. Their heavy tools look like toys in their huge hands. Michelangelo caresses the marble gently, as if he were patting a horse.

"Just perfect!" he says, admiring the block.

Two of the men spit on the ground. Michelangelo does the same. Surprised, Pablo waggles his brown ear.

"Michelangelo had impeccable manners, which he learned when he was living with the dukes. But in the quarry, where he spent a lot of time with the stonemasons, he behaved as they did," Mr. Tonatelli murmurs to you.

"Are you coming back soon, Master Michelangelo?" one of the stonemasons asks, rubbing his nose with the back of his hand.

Michelangelo nods distractedly. He is already thinking about the figure he wants to carve out of the marble. He tilts his head from side to side, narrows his eyes and furrows his brow so wrinkles appear on his forehead.

"Why is he pulling that funny face?" asks the smallest of the stonemasons. Michelangelo overhears his question.

Without taking his eyes from the marble he replies irritably,

"The figure is there in the stone. I just have to set it free. I can see it already."

The stonemasons grin and dig one another in the ribs with their elbows.

Michelangelo gently runs his hand over a sign that has been roughly carved into one side of the marble.

-⟨I⟩ΞV-

17

A continent was discovered 17 years after Michelangelo's birth. Which one?

"No one is allowed to touch any block with your seal on it," the largest stonemason assures him.

The man's neck is so muscular, he looks as if he could lift a heavy car.

Mr. Tonatelli slams the book shut.

"It's not that. That's not what's meant by the seven seals."

The scene that you just saw—and with it, the quarry, the stonemasons and Michelangelo—has disappeared.

A last, shimmering pinch of marble dust dissolves into the air.

Mr. Tonatelli reopens the book, as if he wants to try again.

Under his breath he reads, *"Michelangelo Buonarroti... born on the sixth of March 1475 between two and five o'clock in the morning... in the Italian town of Caprese... on a Monday... star sign Pisces. His father is mayor of the town... He has four brothers... Because his mother is very weak after the birth, he is cared for by a wet nurse, who feeds him. She is the wife of a stonemason...*

Later Michelangelo says, 'I absorbed my skills with a hammer and chisel with my foster mother's milk.'"

Not a word about the seven seals.

From the back of the book comes a stifled cry of pain.

"Ouch! Aaaaahhhh!"

ΛΙ ΙΙΙ Ι(Λ

The Business with the Nose

Mr. Tonatelli's hands are trembling as he leafs through the book. He reaches a page where the paper folds itself with a rustle to form a little chapel. The walls are decorated with pictures painted directly onto the rough plaster. The colors glow as if illuminated by a powerful spotlight, but in fact, the chapel is only lit by a few oil lamps. There's Michelangelo again. He is still young, but he is easily recognizable by his rather prominent ears and angular forehead. He's sitting on a stool, a board on his lap, drawing with a piece of red chalk. A boy about the same age is working next to him. His head is bent low over his board and he is drawing erratically. When he looks up, you can see his twisted expression.

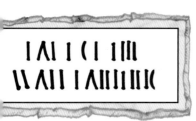

What is Michelangelo drawing?

But why did you hear a cry from this chapter of Michelangelo's life story?

A white-haired man appears behind the two youngsters and peers over their shoulders. He praises Michelangelo's work, but says to the other boy, "Pietro Torrigiano, you'll never make a true master."

The corners of Pietro's mouth twitch with resentment, as if he wants to respond with a scathing remark but bites his tongue.

Michelangelo continues to draw confidently, stroke by stroke.

"He is studying drawing and painting," says Mr. Tonatelli, himself anxious to know what the cry means.

With a bad-tempered snort Pietro Torrigiano lifts his head and, clearly annoyed that his drawing isn't going well, he flings his chalk onto the ground and stomps on it. Michelangelo ignores him. Torrigiano cranes his neck and looks sullenly at the picture that is taking shape. **"You're always sucking up to the teachers,"** Torrigiano says with a sneer. **"You'd crawl through the dirt to lick their boots."** He makes a sign like a worm and gives Michelangelo a sarcastic look.

"Shut up and get lost!" Michelangelo snarls, without stopping his work.

"Don't try to order me about!" Pietro snaps, and jumps up. His drawing board clatters to the ground.

"You're in my way. Move over to one side," Michelangelo demands calmly.

Pietro Torrigiano clenches his fist and strikes out.

"If you want a fight, go outside with the street urchins!"

Michelangelo jeers. He raises his head and smirks quite cruelly.

"Or are you going to beat your drawings out of the paper because you're not doing very well with the chalk."

Pietro slams his fist into Michelangelo's face with all his might. There's a horrible cracking noise.

Michelangelo gives a loud cry. As he grabs his nose, he whimpers softly, rolls his eyes and topples over to one side. His wiry body falls heavily onto the stone floor of the chapel. Torrigiano cannot savor his victory, however. The teacher arrives and starts yelling at him, as he kneels beside the unconscious body of Michelangelo and calls for help.

The picture dissolves and a new scene appears. Michelangelo is being carried away on a wooden stretcher. It looks as though he's dead. Torrigiano is chased out of town.

These events have left Mr. Tonatelli quite breathless.

Pablo whimpers in sympathy and nudges his master with his nose. Mr. Tonatelli quickly pulls a rustling paper bag from his pants pocket and takes out some chocolate drops. Three disappear into his mouth; then he throws one to Pablo, who catches it skillfully between his teeth. Of course he offers you one too.

"Now we know who was responsible for Michelangelo's

broken nose," he says impatiently, *"but we still don't know anything about the secret chamber and the seven seals."*

Disappointed, he closes the book, with the back cover facing upward. For a moment the tiny library is quiet. Pablo whimpers and jumps up on his hind legs as if he wants to take a look at the strange book. Then you hear a noise that sounds like the beating of a huge wing. The back cover of the book has opened by itself. Grayish yellow pieces of parchment flutter out like little birds. They must have been behind the binding. Silently they sway through the air, then slowly they float to the floor, some whirling around like propellers, others spinning like waterwheels.

Pablo catches a piece in his mouth, but he lets go of it immediately, coughing and spitting as if it has left a bitter taste. He keeps wiping his muzzle with his paw.

The ancient scraps of paper now lie between your feet.

On each one there are two or more thick blobs of something dark and hard.

22

A Poisonous Secret

The scraps of paper could be important. Can you find out why?

Pablo backs away with a warning growl. He keeps sticking his tongue out of his mouth, as if he's trying to get rid of the taste.

"The number is no coincidence," Mr. Tonatelli murmurs, and cautiously taps the little pieces of parchment with his toe, as if they might bite.

Pablo growls more loudly.

"Wait here!" Mr. Tonatelli hurries away and, in an instant, returns with a long pair of tweezers and a dented cardboard box in his hands. As he bends down to pick up the scraps of paper, there's a dreadful crunching noise. His face twisted with pain, Mr. Tonatelli drops the tweezers and the box and presses his hand into the small of his back.

"These darned pains," he complains through gritted teeth. Hunched forward, he hobbles down the corridor, but he calls back to you,

"Pick up the scraps of paper and bring them with you!"

Why did he get the tweezers?

"Don't touch them, whatever you do," he warns you from the corridor. It sounds as if they could be poisonous. Mr. Tonatelli struggles down the stairs. With each step he lets out a grunt of pain.

"Come to my office! Pablo will show you the way," he calls from below.

23

The next thing you hear is an outraged *"We're closed. Go away!"*
There's someone in the entrance hall who Mr. Tonatelli is not pleased
to see. It's the woman you met before, when the stone dragon came
to life. This time she looks like an aggressive lizard with its frill raised
as a warning sign. Her dyed orange hair is hanging straight down, and
a small oval hat with a long, curved feather is perched on top of her
head. Under her arm she's carrying a handbag made of crocodile skin.
It's a sad sight because you can still see the crocodile's head. It's biting a
thick metal ring, which forms the clasp of the bag.
Propped lopsidedly on one knee, Mr. Tonatelli looks up
at the woman. She ignores him, however, and waves her
pointed nose around the hall like an antenna searching
for something. Two small figures appear
behind the uninvited guest. At first
glance they look like children, but they
are actually adults—a man and a woman.
With her long, narrow head, the woman reminds
you of a moray eel. The man is a very muscular.
He is bending a metal bar up and down with his hands
as if it were a paper clip.
"Out, Madusa!" Mr. Tonatelli orders angrily, and tries to
force the unwelcome visitor out the door.
Her two companions plant themselves protectively in
front of her. The muscleman threatens Mr. Tonatelli

with the metal bar and the moray eel bares a row of pointed reptilian teeth, unlike anything normally found in a human mouth.

Instead of leaving, Madusa lifts up the crocodile's head and empties her handbag in front of Mr. Tonatelli's worn-out slippers. Sand and small chips of stone fall out.

"What are you waiting for? For the statues to fall off the roof and the monuments to climb off their plinths? Must there be a disaster before you finally move your big backside?"

When Madusa speaks, it sounds like she's spitting.

Pablo comes to his master's aid. Baring his teeth, he stands in front of him and snarls fiercely.

Neither Madusa nor the other two are impressed.

"You are keeping poisonous secrets here. It will be your fault if

disaster befalls the inhabitants of this town. The things you are hoarding in this museum shouldn't be in the hands of a lame old man like you."

Madusa grimaces with disgust, as if Mr. Tonatelli were giving off a foul smell.

Mr. Tonatelli grabs hold of one of the stone pillars to steady himself.

"Get out immediately!" he demands, gasping for breath.

As if he hadn't spoken, the woman gives orders to her companions. *"Ralph, Zitana! The green door at the end of the corridor! Stare at the portrait of Michelangelo. It's a magic picture and will take you back to his time. I want to know everything about the secret chamber and the seven seals."*

Pablo's hackles rise.

Grrrrrr! His snarl sounds as if he wants to tear them both to bits. But it doesn't scare them. Ralph gives him a powerful kick, which sends the poor dog flying across the smooth stone floor. Pablo yelps with shock and lands on his back in the corner.

"Someone has to put an end to this madness!" Madusa explains smugly. Then, with a determined gesture, she pulls up her collar and struts past Mr. Tonatelli.

The Secret of the Seals

"That's it. I'll show the old witch!" you hear the museum owner groan as he gasps for breath.

He motions for you to follow him, before limping to a little door in a dark alcove at the end of the hall.

"Shut the door!" he orders impatiently, and sinks awkwardly into a scuffed leather chair behind a bulky wooden desk. You are in his small office, the floor of which is piled high with books and papers. More are stacked on shelves, which tilt forward under their weight, as if they might collapse in on you at any minute.

Mr. Tonatelli bends over to one side and opens a small door in the wall. Behind it is a bank of switches and levers. The switches and the knobs on the levers look like little devils' heads. Using both hands, Mr. Tonatelli pushes and pulls all the handles into position. Sudden screams echo through the museum. There are creaking and groaning sounds, as if lots of old chests were being shut at the same time. Doors slam, sounding like a drum roll.

"They are locked in, or stuck fast," Mr. Tonatelli tells you with a satisfied cough. *"That Madusa calls herself an alchemist, and she has got her hands on all kinds of magic books. She's been after this museum for a long time, and it's true she knows some of its secrets, but I'd never sell it to her."*

Pablo whimpers, looking for reassurance and wanting you to pet him.

"The pieces of paper. Show me the pieces of paper!" Mr. Tonatelli grabs the box and shakes the scraps of parchment out onto the desk.

> **YOU HAVE SOME PIECES OF PARCHMENT IN YOUR ENVELOPE AT THE BACK OF THE BOOK.**
> **TAKE THEM OUT AND HAVE A LOOK AT THEM!**

Pablo keeps shaking himself, as if he were wet. He sneezes and spits. Mr. Tonatelli glances at him and frowns.

"Pablo can smell something. Something's not quite right with these papers." Mr. Tonatelli slowly struggles to his feet, obviously in great pain. He points to one of the pieces of parchment with a plump finger.

"There... look at that. We recognize that, don't we?"

First Mr. Tonatelli picks up the piece of paper with the tweezers. He examines it from all sides and holds it up to the light from the powerful bulb of his desk lamp.

Which is the right piece of parchment?

The drawings on the parchment look like a picture puzzle, don't they?

Only one symbol has a connection with the head of the faun.

But what do these dark blotches mean?

Mr. Tonatelli's face brightens up.

"Sealing wax. That's sealing wax.

Seven pieces of paper with lots of seals.

It must be a question of finding the right seal."

As Mr. Tonatelli goes to touch the seal next to the picture of the toes, Pablo jumps up and snaps at his wrist. He doesn't bite it hard, he just wants to stop his master.

"Poison!" Mr. Tonatelli exclaims. He looks questioningly down at Pablo, who is anxiously jumping around the legs of his chair.

"You have such a keen nose. You smelled the poison." He moves his finger over to the seal next to the right picture.

Pablo puts his head on one side and wags his tail. He allows Mr. Tonatelli to touch its dark surface.

"Strange sealing wax," Mr. Tonatelli mumbles to himself.

He passes the piece of parchment over to you.

"What do you make of it?"

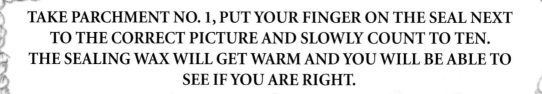

TAKE PARCHMENT NO. 1, PUT YOUR FINGER ON THE SEAL NEXT TO THE CORRECT PICTURE AND SLOWLY COUNT TO TEN. THE SEALING WAX WILL GET WARM AND YOU WILL BE ABLE TO SEE IF YOU ARE RIGHT.

FROM NOW ON, WHENEVER YOU SEE THE ROPE AND THE SEAL, LOOK FOR THE RIGHT PIECE OF PARCHMENT—YOU WILL FIND SOMETHING ON IT THAT YOU HAVE JUST SEEN IN THE BOOK. WARM THE SEAL UNDER THE CORRECT SOLUTION WITH YOUR FINGER FOR TEN SECONDS. MAKE A NOTE OF ALL THE SYMBOLS THAT ARE REVEALED.

Mr. Tonatelli grabs the piece of parchment from your hand and stares at the sign that has appeared. Then he holds the other seals close to the hot lightbulb. Their surface becomes transparent, and skulls appear. But only for a moment. The sealing wax catches fire and a blue flame shoots up, burning a hole in the ancient parchment. Mr. Tonatelli shoves it in a jug half full of water and the fire goes out with a hiss. Black specks float in the water, and the cramped room is filled with the smell of burning. Now it's clear what's supposed to happen.

"You must find the right seals so you can detect the symbols underneath. The trick with the lightbulb is too risky. One of the symbols could catch fire." Mr. Tonatelli draws the first symbol on the pad of paper on his desk. "The symbols will lead us to the secret chamber." He drums his fingers on the desktop.

"There have been rumors in the past of a secret chamber with seven seals. It was said to be the place where Michelangelo's secret was hidden. It could possibly have something to do with the dragon on the roof. We'll have to find out."

The museum owner taps his stomach thoughtfully. "What's trapped in the stone comes to life," he mumbles. Then he explains to you what he means. "My grandfather often told me stories about people who were trapped in stone statues. That's why the statues looked so lifelike. As lifelike as the works of Michelangelo."

Mr. Tonatelli holds the remaining pieces of parchment out toward his dog. "Go on, Pablo, which seals are the right ones and which are poisonous?"

Pablo staggers backward; then his legs give way and he topples over to one side.

He lies there completely motionless.

"Pablo?" Mr. Tonatelli's whole body is trembling. He swallows hard, fighting back the tears. "My Pablo!"

The dog's sides move slightly.

He's still breathing. Pablo is alive, but he must be seriously ill.

"The poison!" Mr. Tonatelli puts both hands down on the desktop and pushes himself up. *"Pablo snapped at a piece of parchment and he had it in his mouth."*

What now? How can the dog be helped?

"Go to the Magic Gallery! Find the portrait of Michelangelo. If you stare into his eyes, you will be caught up in a time vortex that will take you to him!" Mr Tonatelli leans over to the small cabinet in the wall and tries to move all the knobs and switches back to their starting position.

sssSSSparks fly. With a suppressed cry, Mr. Tonatelli tumbles backward and slumps onto the leather chair, forcing the air out of the seat cushion with a sighing ufffl. Blue flashes crackle between the switches and levers, surrounding the cabinet like a glowing spider's web. One of Pablo's ears twitches. At least he's alive.

"The Magic Gallery's out of action." Mr. Tonatelli groans, and then he starts to count up how many other rooms and gadgets have been destroyed. *"Haaa!"* he cries suddenly. Something important must have occurred to him. *"Listen!"*

While the museum owner is talking to you, he pulls open one drawer after another, emptying the contents onto the desk. Soon there's an enormous mountain of papers, handkerchiefs, broken chocolate bars, old newspapers, paper clips, and tattered files towering in front of him. Finally he finds what he's looking for. It's a pile of old drawings.

What are they? Pictures of old cities? There are modern-day postcards among them too.

"There! Rome!" Mr. Tonatelli holds up a faded postcard next to a drawing on a yellowing piece of paper. It looks like a picture of a small town. *"That's what Rome looked like five hundred years ago, when Michelangelo lived there. He was there several times in the service of the pope."*

Mr. Tonatelli presses the drawing into your hand. *"The easel's still working. Up in the studio just under the roof. Let's go! Put the drawing on the easel, take one of the brushes that are there and swirl it around on top of the drawing. The magic easel will transport you to Rome. Look for Michelangelo. Ask him about the poison. He may be able to tell us something."*

The Hooded Man

As time races, so do your feet—which were responsible for bringing you here in the first place. This whole thing seems completely crazy. You look through an open green door, into the gallery where portraits of famous artists are displayed. The legs of Madusa's two assistants are sticking out of one of them, thrashing about furiously. It looks as if the man in the painting is trying to swallow them both.

Madusa herself is trapped between a pair of double doors. Yelling and cursing, she flounders about, struggling to escape, but the doors just grip her more tightly, like a crocodile's jaws, and she can't break free.

Madusa's accomplices couldn't have tracked down Michelangelo. Why not?

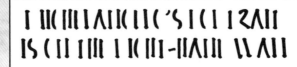

"*I'll make you rich if you'll just help me out of this vise, my dear,*"
she tries to persuade you in a sugary voice.

As you walk past, her sickly sweet expression turns into an evil grimace
and she shouts after you, "*I hope you get warts, and itches in places
you can't scratch.*"

The studio is on the third floor in one of the wings of the museum.
Its sloping walls are made of glass, and reach from the floor right up
to the roof. The rain has made them dull. Picture frames of all sizes
lean against the walls. The room smells of paint and glue, and the acrid
smell of damp cement hangs in the air. There's a single easel standing
in the center of the room. You put the drawing of Rome on it, pick up
one of the paintbrushes, swirl it around and…

Suddenly you feel like you're standing on a skateboard—as if wheels
had sprung from the soles of your shoes. You feel a powerful push from
behind, which sends you flying toward the easel. At first you think
you're going to crash into it, but there's no
impact. Instead, you find yourself
gliding into a tunnel that
stretches out in front
of you. It's not easy
to stay upright!

The tunnel twists and turns as you race deeper and deeper into the drawing. The smell of paint surrounds you—its powerful stench a mixture of dung heap, latrine, and stagnant water, just like a garbage can that hasn't been emptied in ages.

You fall over backward and finish the journey sliding along on your bottom. The ride ends with a bump as you hit solid ground. Your legs crash into a tall, glinting block of white marble. It's worked!

You're back in ancient Rome. The rickety wooden oxcart rattling by proves it.

The block of marble in front of you is one of many. You're surrounded by them. It's as if you've landed in a marble forest. Wherever you look there are rough, often still untrimmed, angular, man-sized blocks.

How many are there? One, two, three, four, five, six, seven, eight, nine, ten, eleven…twenty…thirty…forty…fifty…sixty…seventy…eighty…perhaps even a hundred!

A girl goes by carrying two wicker baskets full of fruit and vegetables. "When on earth is Michelangelo going to build that tomb for Pope Julius the Second? Will he ever carve this stone into statues so we have a bit of space around here again?" she moans to herself.

Behind her is a man wearing coarse pants and a frayed jacket, dragging a heavy sack.

"They're supposed to be forty life-sized figures. But Michelangelo has been collecting the stone here for months and he still hasn't started on them!"

A figure in a dark brown monk's habit squeezes between two blocks of marble. His face is hidden in the shadow of his large cowl, and his long, narrow hands keep disappearing inside his wide sleeves.

"He's a rogue, that Michelangelo," the man says in a falsetto tone, obviously trying to disguise his voice.

That's very interesting. Nowadays Michelangelo is greatly revered.

The man and the girl, who must be servants to rich lords, stop and put down what they are carrying. They look suspiciously at the hooded figure, who clearly wants to keep his face hidden.

"Protect yourselves. Protect yourselves from Michelangelo. He's in league with villains. He's hiding something in a secret chamber that's as dark as his soul," he warns them.

"Tell us more," the two servants demand.

"Have you ever had any dealings with Michelangelo?"

Just the way the man puts the question makes you realize that he doesn't have anything good to say about him.

"A lot of people talk about him." The girl waves her hand meaningfully.

If he's not happy with a statue, he smashes it!

He loves cheese, especially Marzolino cheese from Tuscany.

He's said to be really pigheaded. Stubborn as a mule.

He calls himself a scarecrow because he doesn't like the way he looks.

The man in the cowl gives a little cough of understanding.

"You poor people. If you only knew what Michelangelo is keeping in his secret chamber!"

"What? What is it, then?" The two servants approach the hooded man, eager to hear more, but he backs away and motions to them to keep their distance.

Lowering his voice slyly, he continues, "His statues are very lifelike, aren't they?"

"He's famous. Everyone's talking about him—just like Leonardo da Vinci and Raphael!" the girl says, proud of her knowledge.

"And what if he could turn living beings into stone?"

"That's impossible," the manservant says. "Or is it?" he adds hesitantly.

"There's a reason why Michelangelo has secured his secret chamber with seven seals."

The hooded man turns to leave, but the girl grabs his cowl and holds him back. He pulls her hand away angrily.

"Where is it, this secret chamber?" the girl asks in a whisper.

The hooded man just shrugs his shoulders.

"If he were to drag you there, you'd know all about it," he says threateningly.

The two servants want to find out more, but a horse is racing toward them.

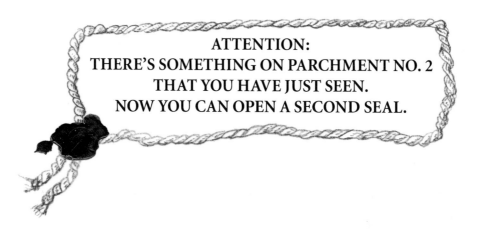

ATTENTION:
THERE'S SOMETHING ON PARCHMENT NO. 2
THAT YOU HAVE JUST SEEN.
NOW YOU CAN OPEN A SECOND SEAL.

Stop, Michelangelo, Stop!

A man gallops by at top speed,
his head stretched forward with fierce
determination. A long cloak hangs from his
shoulders. He urges the horse onward
with his hand. The manservant
cranes his neck and the girl stands
on tiptoe, curious to see where the rider is heading.
Guards in breeches, armed with halberds, swarm from the palace
that towers behind the marble blocks. One of them swings his fist
threateningly at the rider.

"What's going on? Who's that riding away?" the hooded
man asks them sternly.

The guard seems to know who is hiding under the cowl. It must be
someone he holds in great regard. He rushes over to report,
"It's Michelangelo, he's leaving. The pope has decided that he doesn't
want the tomb built after all. Michelangelo is furious.
He's going to Florence and never wants to work for the pope again.
But we're going to chase after him, and we'll catch him."

No wonder Michelangelo was so angry.

It took months to cut and transport all those blocks of marble—each
one is as heavy as a small elephant.

The girl takes an apple from her basket and bites into it.

"That Michelangelo isn't always lucky with his masters."

"What are you talking about?" the other servant asks, taking the apple out of her hand and devouring it in a few quick bites.

"Piero de Medici asked him to build a statue out of snow once. A snowman. If a duke demands something, the artist has to do it if he wants to continue receiving money and living in the palace."

The girl chuckles to herself, pleased that even famous people like Michelangelo are taken advantage of by their masters.

But Michelangelo's departure from Rome means you'll have to go and look for him in Florence. Pablo needs urgent help. But how can you get to Florence? The town is over a hundred miles away, and the only ways to get there are to ride or take a carriage.

And how will you get back to Mr. Tonatelli's museum?

The hooded man has bent down and picked up a piece of marble the size of a fist, which has broken off one of the blocks. His face is pointing toward you, and you hear a rattling snort from the dark shadows of his hood.

That sounds dangerous. The hooded man doesn't seem to like the look of you. Not surprising, really, as you're still wearing your modern clothes. In Rome, five hundred years ago, you must look like an alien.

The hooded man raises his hand, and with an angry shout, he throws the rock at you.

Catch it!

Yes! The rough stone is lying in your hands.

A bony finger points toward you.

"A spy! A villain! A messenger from the devil!" the hooded man exclaims.

The two servants stare at you as if you have horse's hooves and glowing eyes. The manservant shouts for the guards, who come running out of the palace, their halberds raised.

Run! You don't have much time!

There's a sucking sound behind you. The tunnel has opened up again and is rotating like the drum of a washing machine. One step inside is enough. Its spinning knocks you off your feet. The tunnel rears up and turns into a chute, which corkscrews into the ground.

As you *speeeeeeeeeed* along, the chute seems to be glowing underneath your bottom. The heat becomes unbearable and the air is as hot as an oven. Then you reach the end of the chute.

You free-fall into a light room onto a hard floor. *Aaaaaaaaaaaaaaaaaaaa*

WHAAMMMM!

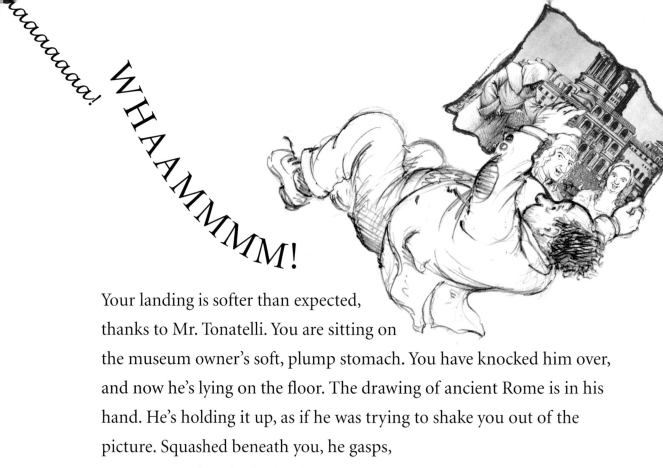

Your landing is softer than expected, thanks to Mr. Tonatelli. You are sitting on the museum owner's soft, plump stomach. You have knocked him over, and now he's lying on the floor. The drawing of ancient Rome is in his hand. He's holding it up, as if he was trying to shake you out of the picture. Squashed beneath you, he gasps,

"You're lucky that I love eating. My stomach saved you."

How does he know this? You have to help him to his feet. He is still standing lopsidedly because his back hurts so much.

"You arrived too late. Michelangelo was already leaving." he says, depressed. *"We need a new plan."*

YOU CAN SEE THE SECRET MESSAGE
THE INNOCENT SERVANTS IN THE FRAME.

**JUST A MINUTE! STOP!
BEFORE YOU GO ANY FURTHER YOU CAN
OPEN ANOTHER SEAL. LOOK AT PARCHMENT NO. 3
AND THINK ABOUT WHAT THE SERVANT GIRL SAID.**

To the Quarry

The chunk of marble is still in your hand. It is roughly hewn, so it is not as smooth and shiny as dressed and polished marble.

Mr. Tonatelli notices the stone and takes it from you. He sniffs it, just as Pablo would.

"From one of the blocks that Michelangelo picked out," you hear him say. *"That means it can lead you to him."*

How?

A walking stick with a silver knob in the form of a lion's head is leaning against the wall. Supporting himself on the stick, Mr. Tonatelli leaves the studio. He carries on talking as he walks.

"A few things in the museum have started working again."

When you get to the doors that are holding Madusa, like a guard dog would a burglar, you are met with a volley of abuse.

"Open them, you stubborn old walrus! I'll pay you back for this, and it will be a lot worse than your lumbago."

47

Mr. Tonatelli just waves her aside, taking no notice of the uninvited visitor.

"It's going to be a squeeze," he warns you. *"I could never get in there myself."* He strokes his belly with his free hand, *"I'd get stuck like a cork in a bottle."* When you arrive at the entrance hall, he stops and points to the pillars with the end of his stick.

"Touch them!"

What? Why should you do that?

He gestures impatiently with his stick, urging you to get on with it. So you stretch out your hands and run them over the smooth surfaces of the stone pillars. They are made of red, green and white marble, with dark veins running through them.

Interesting! The pillars all feel cold to the touch except the one closest to the museum owner's office, which is warm.

Mr. Tonatelli is pleased.

"You found it!" he exclaims, banging his stick triumphantly on the ground. *"You noticed the difference. Now you know how to tell a real marble pillar from a fake one. Real marble always feels cold to the touch. If the pillar is made of wood, and just painted to look like marble, it feels warm."*

Then he remembers that you're supposed to be looking for Michelangelo and you need to find him urgently. *"Jump!"* he shouts. What does he mean?

"Jump!" Mr. Tonatelli urges you. Your confused face makes him

48

angry. *"What an idiot I am!"* he says to himself and goes over to the fake marble pillar. He looks up at it, then hobbles around it, searching for something. *"First we have to get rid of the pillar. Where's the opening mechanism?"*

Then he turns to you. *"You must go to the quarry in Siena. No, Lucca. No, the one at Montepulciano, or was it Carrara? The name must be here somewhere. Can you find it? My eyes aren't what they used to be."*

The name of the right place is shown on the pillar.
The letters may be
hidden — , or | or / .

"Press the letters, one after another," Mr. Tonatelli demands.

The stone buttons grate and they're difficult to push into the pillar.

It's **haaaaaaaaaard** work.

But it's worth it. There's yet another surprise in this museum. You hear a squeak in the ceiling above your head, then a loud rattling and rumbling. The pillar rises, as if pulled up by heavy chains, to reveal a round hole in the floor.

"Throw the piece of marble in!" Mr. Tonatelli instructs nervously.

Is there a stream down there?

The piece of marble  … and lands with a… THUD!

You lean over the edge. Light is streaming up from below. Bright sunlight, as if there were another world beneath you, rather than water or a cellar.

"Jump! You can't come to any harm!"

Mr. Tonatelli must have gone mad. He pushes you into the hole and you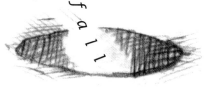

-S-SS-Ƈ

You hear Pablo barking up above. Has he recovered? Or does he need your help even more?

The Runaway Block

This is how an angel must feel, falling to earth.

As soon as your legs hit the bright daylight at the end of the deep shaft, you slow down. You float the last few yards, while getting a bird's-eye view of a big quarry. Stone blocks are being hewn from the rock as if giants were at work, making dice for a game.

Extraordinary! Really extraordinary! This was happening five hundred years ago, when there were no explosives or pneumatic drills.

So how did men cut these enormous blocks, some twice or three times as big as they were, out of the mountain?

The air in the quarry is filled with the banging of numerous hammers, the scraping of chisels and the shouts of the men. Madness!

Because there were no trucks then, the marble blocks are hauled down on sleds made of several tree trunks bound together.

One is rumbling down the earthy slope now, grinding and crunching as small pieces of stone fly about to either side of it.

Nine men are holding strong ropes attached to the back of the sled to stop it from hurtling down the slope.

"What on earth are you?"

Who spoke?

For goodness' sake! Your shoes haven't touched the ground yet. They're still a good few feet in the air.

Beneath you stands a small figure, shading his eyes against the glaring sun with his hand and staring straight at you. At first sight he comes across like a ghost. Two piercing blue eyes look out from his powdery white face. His hair, hands, tattered shirt and frayed pants are also encrusted with a thick layer of white dust. Finally your feet touch the ground. But it's certainly no ghost that digs you hard in the side with his finger. His small mouth grins at you, revealing several missing teeth.

"You're such a prankster! Carrying on like that, pretending you can fly!"

On the slope above you, the men are still struggling with the block of marble. The ropes are groaning under the strain and the men gasp with the effort. The wooden sled slides forward, then skids over to one side.

"Tighter! Hold it tighter," yells one of the men.

A rope breaks with a dull snap and the end flicks back, hitting the man who was holding it in the head. He falls to the ground with a groan.

Then the sled breaks as the ropes that were holding the tree trunks together wear through.

The tree trunks act as rollers, and the block of marble plunges down toward the valley. The boy next to you, who owes his ghostly appearance to the marble dust, stares spellbound at the giant lump of stone.

Like an armor-plated prehistoric monster, the block hurtles down, then topples over the edge of the ramp of earth, heading straight for you.

Jump aside!
Out of the way!

The ground beneath your feet shakes and trembles. Dark dust rises like a storm cloud. Splinters of wood, sharp-edged chips of stone, and lumps of earth fill the air. The boy stares at the terrible spectacle as if in a trance. He's right in the path of the block of marble. You must pull him out of the way. Grab his arm. **Move!** **Move!** **Move!**

You land in a dried-up bush that clings to the hillside by its roots, so breaking your fall.

The block of marble rumbles past just a few feet away. It reaches the bottom of the slope, where the ground is flat, and stops.

A ghostly silence settles over the quarry.

The anxious cry of a man echoes from the rock walls.

"DONATELLA? ARE YOU THERE, DONATELLA?"

The dusty figure next to you coughs and splutters.

"You're not a prankster, you're an angel! You saved my life!" she says, her voice thick with dust. Her wide, bright blue eyes look at you as if she's seen a ghost.

So the boy is a girl in boy's clothes.

"Father will tell me off. I'm not supposed to be here with the stonemasons. He has forbidden it."

Donatella hides behind you as the men go past, muttering and cursing. It's going to be terribly hard work for them to pull the block back up to the road leading to the river. It has to be transported by boat.

They don't notice you. The stonemasons are too busy looking at the marble block.

Donatella gives you a grateful bow, her hands clasped together.

Has she seen Michelangelo? She nods eagerly.

"He was here a couple of weeks ago!"

That's not much help to you.

"Someone else was here, asking about him!" Donatella fidgets excitedly and draws a long, hooded robe in the air with her hands. *"I never saw his face, but his voice was really harsh."* Although the girl is anything but a coward, she shudders. *"Even the stonemasons crossed themselves when the hooded man came."*

But what was he doing at the quarry?

Donatella looks around in case anyone might overhear her.

"He talked about a secret cave. It's supposed to be locked and secured with seals."

Michelangelo's secret chamber. So it's in the marble quarry. But where? Donatella apologizes sheepishly, because she doesn't know.

"But I can find out, ready for when you float down from the sky again. You can come back and protect me."

It's best if you say nothing.

A short distance away a man is dragging a tree trunk with a few branches and some dried silvery leaves.

"They're going to pry out a new block," Donatella explains quickly, pleased to be able to tell you something.

She leads you higher up the mountain to show you how it's done. First they find a long vein that runs through the rock; then they chisel a deep groove in it. Wedges of olive wood are put in the groove and sprinkled with water.

The wood begins to swell and exerts tremendous force.

55

The pressure along the length of the vein pushes the marble block away from the mountain.

YOU CAN OPEN ANOTHER SEAL.
LOOK AT PARCHMENT NO. 4.

A deep voice calls from the clouds, *"Have you found him?"* Donatella lets go of your arm, gulps a few times and looks up at the sky, completely awestruck.

"Have you come for me? Are you the angel of death? Has God sent you?" she asks.

There's no point in telling her about the Museum of Adventures and the deep shaft.

"To get back, just throw a piece of marble in the air!"

You'd better return to the museum. You can come back to the quarry later. So you pick up a lump of marble and throw it in the air!

56

The Birds of Death Are Calling

Good news!

An unseen force pulls you out of the round shaft and drops you onto the stone floor of the entrance hall. You find yourself squatting in front of Pablo, who licks your cheeks eagerly with his rough tongue. He jumps up at you, pushing you over backward, then stands on your stomach, wagging his tail happily and behaving as if you've been gone for months.

"The poison's stopped working," Mr. Tonatelli reports with relief, and swallows a few chocolate buttons to keep him going. Pablo proves that he's fully recovered by immediately begging for a chocolate.

Bad news!

"Madusa has managed to free herself. Her two little cronies have escaped too!" Mr. Tonatelli mops the sweat from his brow with a checked handkerchief. *"I'm sure they're still in the museum, but I can't find them anywhere."*

There are three pieces of parchment left. Three seals still to open. You should have tracked down the secret chamber in the quarry.

Still limping, Mr. Tonatelli heads out of the building and struggles down the steps. The poor man! He stands there, bent over like the letter C, studying the stone dragons on the edge of the roof.

You and Pablo follow him.

The gray statues look rigid and aloof.

A stiff breeze sweeps through the square, driving black clouds across the sky above your heads. Although it's early afternoon, it seems to be getting dark.

Stone owls crouch at the corners of the roof. All four, six, or perhaps even more, throw their heads back at the same time. The heads don't appear to be attached to their bodies. Suddenly they spin around in a circle, open their beaks and call in unison,

TWIT! TWIT! TWOOO!

Madusa flies through the open doors of the museum, her cloak fanned out around her, as if she's been lifted up by a strong gust of wind. She throws her head back and starts to laugh. The sound reminds you of breaking glass.

Slowly she comes down the steps, staring at you with eyes as large and round as those of the owls. Her skin has a poisonous yellow hue with glimmering green spots.

"Tonatelli, you fool!"

Why is she laughing like that?

"Do you hear the call of the birds of death? Their cry means someone will die soon!" Madusa's bony index finger points to Mr. Tonatelli, then to you and finally down at Pablo.

"Who will it be? You? You? Or him?"

Mr. Tonatelli, who is normally so self-assured, clasps his hand to his heart and pants for breath. *"Stop talking like that, Madusa!"* he gasps.

She takes no notice of him. Instead, she twirls around. Her cloak flies up and hits you in the face.

"The dragon is alive!" Her voice is a shrill screech against the noise of the storm rumbling above the museum.

She's right!

Two gray wings are unfolding on the stone porch over the entrance. They spread out as if trying to reach out to the corners of the museum.

The dragon opens its mouth, exposing two rows of pointed teeth.

Now the dragon bellows. It's a sharp cry that makes Pablo jump into your arms. Then his courage returns and he starts barking furiously in the direction of the monster. His whole body is quivering.

The dragon takes off from the porch, and its gigantic dark gray shadow heads straight for you.

You are able to run away, but Mr. Tonatelli can't move so fast.

The stone creature, which has suddenly come to life, threatens to hit him. Madusa, who is standing within easy reach of him, doesn't move. She simply leans over to one side as the statue glides away just above her head.

It makes a rustling sound louder than the leaves of a thousand-year-old oak in a storm. Making use of the updraft, the dragon zigzags upward on the storm gusts, climbs high into the sky and disappears out of view behind the glass facade of an office block.

Madusa's manner has changed completely. Full of dark foreboding, she stares after the stone creature.

"It will bring death to the town. And it will be your fault, Tonatelli!" With great difficulty, his face racked with pain, the museum owner straightens up.

"Your museum is the gateway to the dark powers of the underworld. It doesn't belong in the hands of a blockhead like you," she continues. Pablo tears across the pavement and barks until he is blue in the face. He's barking at the roof of the museum, where the stone owls have adopted their normal rigid position again.

Then Madusa does something strange. She puts her thumb up behind her back, as if she wants to let someone know that everything is okay.

Who was the sign meant for?

Why did she direct it toward the museum?

With an accusing look, Madusa puts her fingers in her ears.

"Make that dog shut up!" she demands angrily. Then she sticks her chin out and stalks off.

But where are her assistants, Ralph and Zitana?

Mr. Tonatelli brandishes his walking stick and tries to think of something to shout after her.

As he can't come up with anything better, he yells, *"You green swamp gherkin!"*

Follow the Golden Path

The storm breaks over the museum. The first heavy drops of rain splash onto the asphalt, leaving large, ragged blotches. You and Mr. Tonatelli run into the building. Pablo is still barking, as if he's trying to set a world record. He races to the staircase and wants to go upstairs, but then he runs back over to you and taps the ground with his paws.

What's he trying to tell you?

Mr. Tonatelli drums his fingers on his stomach and ponders.

"Only Michelangelo himself can tell us the truth about his secret chamber. You must speak to him."

Back in his office, Mr. Tonatelli fiddles about in every nook and cranny, and for a while all you hear from him is *"Not working. Not yet. Must fix it. It's faulty."* In between, he keeps saying, *"I don't believe it!"* Pablo is standing on the first step of the staircase up to the next floor and growls. What's up there?

Mr. Tonatelli returns with a large key ring in his hand. Long, old-fashioned keys dangle from it.

"I haven't been there for a long time, but it's our best hope of finding him!"

What he means by this remains a mystery. He gestures impatiently for you and Pablo to follow him. He leads you via some back stairs into an overgrown garden. The rain doesn't seem to bother him.

He is heading for a gate made of black wrought-iron bars, surrounded by wild roses. Through the bars you can see a small pool filled with reeds and duckweed, which occupies the rear part of the garden.

"We must find the right key." Mr. Tonatelli holds up one after the other. They all look very unusual. Such keys only lock old gates and doors. The keys are shaped in a way you've never seen before.

"Which is the key to Michelangelo?"

The lock grates as Mr. Tonatelli turns the key.

An ancient mechanism that hasn't been oiled for many years snaps into place and pushes the latch to one side.

The heavy hinges of the barred gate screech—as loudly and off-key as the worst singer in your class.

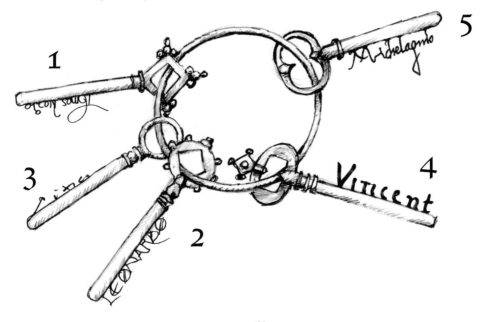

The pain in your ears is soon forgotten when you look into the garden. The gnarled trees no longer stand behind the gate. The pond has disappeared. Instead, you see a vast plain bathed in golden light.

"Michelangelo is the best sculptor in the world," Mr. Tonatelli says, his voice full of respect. He beckons to you. *"His most famous statues will appear if you follow the golden path."*

As he says this, gleaming paving stones spring from the sandy ground, forming a winding path that reaches from your shoes to the horizon.

"Keep walking along the path. Pablo will go with you. You can only speak to Michelangelo once. You must pick a moment when he will listen to what you have to say and answer you. Don't do it when he's immersed in his work."

Although it's still raining all around you, a warm breeze blows through the barred gate. Pablo puts his paws cautiously onto the golden path, as if it might cave in at any minute. Step by step, you feel your way through this unfamiliar land. When you turn around, you see an archway behind you, where Mr. Tonatelli is standing in the dark-green, rain-soaked garden. He carefully closes the barred gate. The lock clicks into place.

Freed from the Stone

On your left-hand side, the sand swirls around as if it's caught up in a whirlwind.

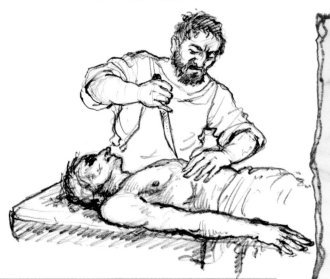

Michelangelo is fascinated by the human body. He is allowed to dissect corpses in the cellar of a hospital, where he examines every muscle and tendon to learn how each interacts. The stench that surrounds him is dreadful and often leaves him unable to eat or drink. But he puts up with it, just to find out the secrets of the body.

This relief is one of his first works. The figures are fighting with great determination. Apparently Michelangelo loved this carving so much that it always hung on the wall of his studio.

When he was twenty years old, Michelangelo created a sleeping cupid that he wanted to sell as an ancient Greek statue, so he buried it for a while. He sold it to a cardinal, who really believed that it came from Greece and was two thousand years old. Michelangelo's deception was found out, but he was lucky—he wasn't charged or imprisoned; instead, people marveled that he had made such a convincing copy of a Greek statue.

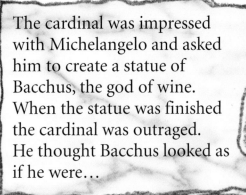

The cardinal was impressed with Michelangelo and asked him to create a statue of Bacchus, the god of wine. When the statue was finished the cardinal was outraged. He thought Bacchus looked as if he were…

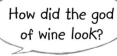

How did the god of wine look?

65

Michelangelo used various tools. Using a pointed chisel, he removed large chunks of stone. With the toothed chisel, he carved the shape out of the hard marble. For fine details, he used the chisel with the smooth blade. Then he smoothed the stone with rasps and files.

Some of Michelangelo's statues are smooth and polished; others still show the marks of the chisels.

He always carved all his figures out of a single block. He never put several blocks together, as did other sculptors at the time.

ϽIIレϽՐ

They must look alive!

Michelangelo didn't complete all his statues. But here you can see how he brought the figures out of the rock.

If Michelangelo struck a dark vein in the marble while he was working, he sometimes destroyed the whole statue. On one occasion he wanted to carve a hand. When he came to a dark area in the marble, he changed his plan. Instead of the hand, he created an angry mask, then he positioned the figure's arm behind its back.

Michelangelo was just twenty-four years old when he created the statue of the Virgin Mary with the body of Jesus on her lap. Jesus looks as if he's asleep, and Mary is not just grieving, she seems to be contemplating the sacrifice Jesus made for mankind. Look at the folds in her clothes—they look as if they're made of fabric, not solid marble.

Let me tell you a secret. Michelangelo played a little trick with their proportions. If they were to stand side by side, they'd look like this.

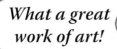

What a great work of art!

An artist from Pisa is said to have created it.

When Michelangelo heard that, he secretly returned in the night and chiseled his name in the sash across the Virgin Mary's chest.

MICHAEL·ANGELUS·
BONAROTUS·FLORENT·
FACIEBAT

Translated, this means:
Michelangelo Buonarroti
from Florence made this.

**LOOK AT PARCHMENT NO. 5.
YOU CAN OPEN ANOTHER SEAL.**

David

The golden path suddenly leads you through the alleyways of a town. The paving stones lose their shine and become gray. The yellowish gray, pale pink and greenish white plastered houses stand very close together. A bridge, lined with a row of small shops, stretches across a wide, slow-flowing river. A street trader selling melons is shouting at the top of his voice.

Michelangelo's idea has been accepted by the city council. But what on earth is he carving out of the marble?

Today we're finally going to see it.

Michelangelo has worked on it for two winters and three summers. There's a wooden screen around the statue.

It's supposed to be a symbol of the city's strong defenses. Florence has withstood so many attackers.

"The best in Florence!" he cries.

You are in the town where Michelangelo lived for many years. Maybe you'll meet him now.

All sorts of things are being sold on the bridge, from shimmering cloth to carved bowls and silver chalices. Trinkets are for sale too. But most of the citizens hardly have eyes for the merchandise; they are rushing to the houses in the town.

A ragged dog goes by with a large bone between his teeth. Pablo licks his lips. He'd like to get hold of that bone. The people are chattering excitedly. There's tension in the air, like just before a big football match.

There's a fierce argument raging in one of the alleyways that the people are heading for. The cause is a brick archway that stretches from one side to the other, linking two houses. Men with heavy iron hammers are standing on ladders, ready to demolish the arch. A thin man is shouting and shaking the ladder.

Losing his temper, the man flings his cap onto the ground and tramples on it. "You're not going to destroy anything here! This David can stay where he is, so far as I'm concerned. I don't want him!" The man on the ladder spits into his hand. "Master Michelangelo wants the statue erected in the square, but it won't fit through your archway, so we'll have to knock it down." "No, no, no, you oafish louts!" The man's head is blood red and looks as if it's ready to explode. His rants fall on deaf ears. Their hammers are already thundering against the stone, and the archway collapses. Pablo climbs over the debris and barks at you. He wants you to follow him.

As you round the corner, you see that things are even worse. Where the alleyway is too narrow, part of a house has been ripped away. Farther on there's a loud uproar. Noisy shouts of "Bravo!" are mixed with fierce curses and outraged cries. The white marble statue towers over the heads of the townspeople. It's the figure of a young man. It's moving forward in little jerks. The plinth is standing on a timber framework, which is being rolled along on tree trunks stripped of their bark.

Lots of people seem to like this statue of David, but some are very upset about his nudity.

How heavy do you think such a statue would be? The same as a car, a truck or two elephants?

Although the men who are transporting it have wide shoulders and powerful muscles, they are finding it very difficult to move.

The setting sun spreads a copper-red glow over the roofs of the houses. Guards with helmets and lances push their way through the crowd and station themselves around the statue to guard it. The people's anger could erupt, and they might try to damage the statue.

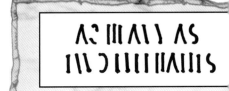

David is carrying a slingshot over his shoulder. You can see every tiny detail of his face and body.

Michelangelo has even created the blood vessels under his skin out of marble.

Today David is as world-famous as the *Mona Lisa*.
But Michelangelo has not appeared. Where can you find him?

Moses Has Horns!

Where's Pablo? Why has he left your side?

Something heavy lands on your toes. Is Michelangelo nearby?

Has he dropped his hammer? The sharp pain in your big toe makes you cringe.

But it's not a hammer you find lying at your feet, it's a bone. A bone so huge it looks as if it's come from an elephant, or a dinosaur! Pablo has dragged it here and is looking at it proudly. His tongue is hanging out of his mouth and he's panting heavily. It must have been very difficult for him to carry. But who did he steal it from?

Golden beams of light pierce the dust of the alley, reaching up to the sky like long needles. A rustling gust of wind sweeps around the corner and uncovers another section of the golden path.

Pairs of eyes flash at you from the end of the street. Many pairs of eyes. Deep growls echo through the night air. Pablo immediately hides between your legs and tries to make himself as small as possible. He puts his paws over his eyes. He seems to think that if he can't see anything, no one can see him.

Now it's obvious who the bone belonged to. The town's dogs have banded together to teach this trespasser a lesson. Crouching low, they creep nearer.

Quick, run! With any luck they won't be able to follow you onto the golden path. Pablo races ahead, with you right behind him. But now the pack of dogs are heading toward you, led by a shaggy, dark gray monster that looks like a cross between a calf and a bear.

Run, run, run!

Barking wildly, the dogs chase after you.

The distance between you and them is shrinking frighteningly fast.

The buildings of Florence fade to a mist, which dissolves in the light from the path. The barking grows quieter. The dogs are jumping up against an invisible wall. They bounce off it and, puzzled, fall back on their hindquarters. Pablo realizes that he's safe and makes a noise that sounds like a mocking snort. Then he remembers the bone he had to leave behind in Florence and whimpers sadly. But something else has appeared on the path ahead. Two men in heavy velvet robes are standing in front of you, bowing their heads with respect.

"So that's what the tomb of Pope Julius the Second looks like," one of them says admiringly.

Julius the Second? He's the pope who wanted a tomb with forty statues. But when he suddenly changed his mind, Michelangelo left Rome in a rage. Now it looks as if the tomb has been completed after all, but it's quite a bit smaller.

A dark brown monk's habit comes into view, like a shadow warning of evil. Again, all you can see inside the cowl is darkness. Does this stranger actually have a face? The hooded man stands next to the pair admiring the tomb, which is as tall as a two-story building. He raises one baggy sleeve and points to the large central figure. "𝕯𝖔𝖊𝖘𝖓'𝖙 𝖍𝖊 𝖑𝖔𝖔𝖐 𝖑𝖎𝖐𝖊 𝖙𝖍𝖊 𝖉𝖊𝖛𝖎𝖑 𝖍𝖎𝖒𝖘𝖊𝖑𝖋?" the hooded man asks, as if the only possible answer is 'yes.'

One of the noble gentlemen looks at him suspiciously, then leans backward, as if he doesn't want to get too close.
"It's a statue of Moses carrying the tablets bearing the Ten Commandments," the first man says.

"His face reminds me of Master Michelangelo. I think he wanted to immortalize himself here," the other adds.

The long sleeve conceals a fist, which is raised threateningly.

"Can't you see the horns on his head? Michelangelo has portrayed Moses as a figure from hell!"

The men just laugh contemptuously at this remark.

"That's not Michelangelo's fault. Many people have made the same mistake in translating the holy text. It states that Moses came down from Mount Sinai with the two tablets of testimony and rays of light beaming from his head, but it was mistranslated as 'horns on his head.' That's the only reason why Michelangelo carved him like that."

Irritated, the hooded man turns away with a snort. He swishes off as if his feet aren't touching the ground.

The two men watch him go, shaking their heads; then they turn back to the tomb.

As he slowly disappears into the distance, you hear one of them say,

"Many people are envious of someone as brilliant and successful as Michelangelo. How stupid to speak ill of the great artist."

Be warned, Michelangelo!

You have reached the end of the golden path. A wide, shimmering plain stretches in front of you in every direction. Pablo turns around in a circle and whimpers, as if asking where you should go.

There's a gentle crunch in the glittering sand. The surface ripples like seawater. Pablo pricks up his ears. He finds the noise disturbing. Prancing around in a circle, he is waiting for what is to come.

Walls suddenly shoot up from the ground like a giant fountain. The sand sprays outward—not a single grain lands inside on the light and dark marble.

Two walls form a right angle; then a third blocks you in. The fourth wall forces Pablo outside, and then a domed roof slides over the top. You are standing alone in a hall inlaid with marble from floor to ceiling. Figures recline on stone tombs against two of the walls—a man and a woman in both cases. The marble is many different colors—dark gray distinguishes the pillars and arches, white lights up the walls and the statues themselves glow sandy yellow. It's utterly peaceful here. Even the statues seem to be entranced, half lost in contemplation, reflecting, dreaming. Is this a burial vault? Are you underground?

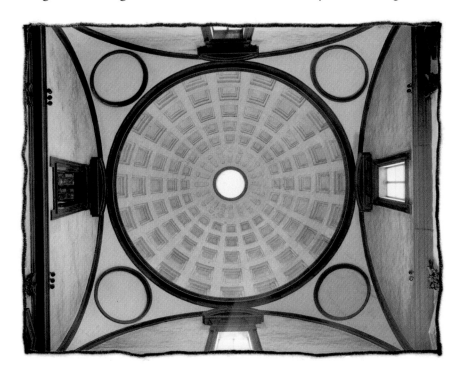

An elaborate cupola with windows, columns and circles soars above your head. Looking up is like looking through a kaleidoscope.

A heavy wooden door with square panels opens and a man comes in. He looks similar to the Moses statue. Is this Michelangelo?

The hooded man appears behind him in the half-open door.

"𝔚𝔥𝔞𝔱 𝔞 𝔟𝔢𝔞𝔲𝔱𝔦𝔣𝔲𝔩 𝔠𝔥𝔞𝔭𝔢𝔩!" he says admiringly, but it sounds affected and insincere.

The other man—who could be Michelangelo himself—nods without turning around. He doesn't know who he's talking to.

"The chapel of the Medici family. Some of them have found everlasting peace here. I took great pleasure in designing it—not just the figures, the whole chapel."

You're standing right in front of Michelangelo. He's bound to notice you. Can't he see you? Michelangelo points to two of the reclining figures. They represent Dawn and Dusk.

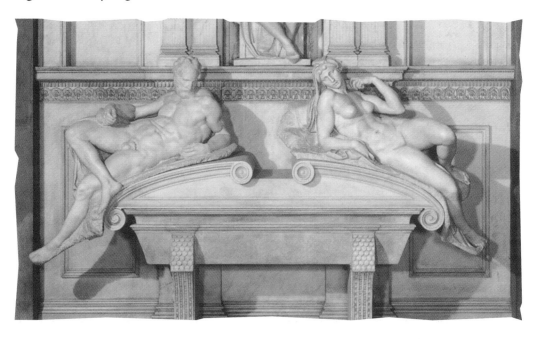

These two represent Day and Night.
The hooded man lays his hand on the artist's shoulder. Michelangelo swings around—not shocked, but outraged at this lack of respect. He straightens up when he sees the faceless figure.

"Who are you?" he demands angrily.

The hooded man doesn't reply. He moves threateningly toward Michelangelo, who backs away.

"I know your darkest secrets. Beware! You will never play a part in building the most magnificent cathedral in the world. St. Peter's Cathedral will still be standing long after your statues have decayed. Everyone will revere the name of the architect, Bramante."

Who is Day and who is Night? Which of the figures doesn't seem to be finished?

THE WOMAN IS DAY AND THE MAN IS LAZY. HIS HEAD IS NOT FINISHED.

Michelangelo cringes when he hears this name.
"So don't even dare think that your ideas could be useful in the construction of St. Peter's." The hooded man puts his hands on Michelangelo's chest and gives him a shove.

Michelangelo stumbles backward. He tries to grab hold of the hooded man, but the man whirls around and disappears out the door. The door slams and the crash echoes fourfold off the smooth walls.

Michelangelo stands there, glowering. He looks in your direction, but he seems to see straight through you.

You are just a time traveler. You can watch, but you can't speak.

The chapel fades and finally disappears completely, together with Michelangelo.

Pablo rushes over to you and stands at your feet.

How are you supposed to find out about the secret chamber? And which poison the sealing wax on the pieces of parchment contains? And what about Michelangelo's supposed secrets?

NOW YOU CAN OPEN SEAL NO. 6.

Pablo's Discovery

You must hurry!

You follow the golden path back to where you started.

Mr. Tonatelli is waiting for you at the wrought-iron gate.

He's dripping wet.

His teeth are chattering as he hobbles back into the museum with you and Pablo. Once Pablo has shaken himself briskly, he stretches his head in the direction of the second floor and pricks up his ears.

A flash of lightning streaks across the sky, and the trees in front of the window turn white. Thunderclaps rumble overhead like cannon shots. They have no effect on Pablo. He barks as if he's gone out of his mind and races up to the second floor, three steps at a time. Pressing his hands into his aching back, Mr. Tonatelli stares after him, bewildered.

"He usually hides in the wastepaper basket during a storm!"

It can only mean one thing. Something's wrong upstairs in the museum.

A strange bell tinkles. It sounds like a cowbell in an Alpine meadow. It turns out to be the front door bell, hanging next to the door on the inside, which can be rung from outside by pulling on a vertical black metal bar. It rings a second, then a third time.

Mr. Tonatelli shuffles off to open the door, without letting the staircase out of his sight.

Pablo's barking is getting quieter. Where has he run off to?

Three policemen are standing at the door, shaking the rain from their caps and uniform jackets. The tallest of the three runs a hand over his angular chin—he doesn't seem to know quite how to begin.

"So," he says slowly, "do you know someone called Madusa?"

Mr. Tonatelli hisses like an overheated pressure cooker.

"I've had enough of her! Leave me in peace!"

"She came to see us because...because..." The policeman rocks backward and forward on his toes.

"Because the stone dragon flew away? We're trying to find out how that happened. It must have something to do with Michelangelo's seven seals," Mr. Tonatelli babbles. *"And the little owls on the roof were hooting as well. Did you catch it?"*

The policemen stares at the museum owner, completely at a loss.

"Catch what?"

"The stone dragon that flew away!"

Suddenly Madusa appears in the doorway.

She has been caught in the rain too.

Wet strands of hair are stuck to her face.

"There, did you hear that?" she says to the policeman with the closely cropped beard.

"He's gone mad. Or have you heard of stone creatures that come to life?"

"No, no, no!" The three policemen shake their heads in unison.

"To be honest, this museum is crumbling. The statues just fell off the roof. They might have hit someone, but this fathead likes to fantasize about flying stone dragons." Full of contempt, she stares at Mr. Tonatelli's round stomach and turns up her nose. As if further proof were necessary, at this moment something crashes onto the steps and smashes into pieces. It must be one of the many gargoyles that stare out from the edge of the roof.

"There!" With a gesture as if to say "I told you so!" Madusa blinks, seemingly bored with the whole thing. Mr. Tonatelli snorts through both nostrils.

"You'll stop at nothing to get rid of me, you monster!"

A shrill cry comes from the staircase. "Let go of me, you mutt!" At once Madusa's face turns as gray and hard as stone. Growling fiercely, Pablo is dragging someone down the stairs. It's the woman who looks like a moray eel.

87

Her arms are flailing as she tries to find something to grab hold of. Her companion is lurching down awkwardly behind her. The muscles in his thighs are so big that he has to swing his legs out to the sides when he walks. Hanging around his neck is a little box with switches and tiny joysticks. Things seem to fall into place.

What is the man carrying?

What Really Happened

The eel-faced woman and the muscleman have left a damp trail on the stairs. They are both completely soaked through.

"It's all Zitana's fault, boss. She must think she's made of sugar, the stupid fool. She insisted on coming in out of the rain. I would have stayed on the roof."

"It's not true, not true!" the moray eel retorts. Pablo is still hanging on to her arm. He's not prepared to loosen his grip.

"Ralph is petrified of storms. He's such a wimp!"

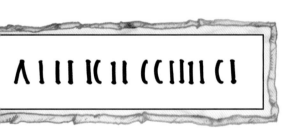

Madusa's nose seems to grow longer and more pointed. *"I've never seen these two before in my life,"* she snaps abruptly, and bats her eyelids. *"They're just riffraff— the sort of people that are always imposing themselves on others. Nothing more."*

88

Furious, Ralph stalks over to her.

"I'll tie a knot in your bones, you ungrateful witch. Do you think we're doing your dirty work just so you can pretend you don't know us?"

Things don't look good for Madusa. The tall policeman adopts a serious expression, while his colleagues move to block her escape.

"May I ask you for an explanation?" he asks politely.

Before Madusa can say anything, Ralph starts talking.

"We were told to put these remote-controlled figures up on the roof. We substituted them for the real stone statues."

There's a sound of cloth ripping. Pablo has torn off a large piece of Zitana's jacket. He spits it out and grabs the woman by the ankle.

Trying to wriggle free, she whines, **She's determined to get her hands on this museum, that so-called witch. She's about as capable of casting a spell as I am of becoming a giant."**

"Willful damage to property," the policeman states. "You're coming with us. Disturbing the peace. Public order offenses. You're in serious trouble, madam."

Once a policeman has hold of the eel-faced woman, Pablo is willing to release her. He hasn't harmed her, but he's proud to have caught the two intruders at last.

As the police drive away, Mr. Tonatelli pushes the door closed and leans back against it. The rain is still pattering outside, but the rumbling of the storm is moving farther away.

"So the secret chamber and the seven seals were a red herring,"

Mr. Tonatelli says, sounding disappointed.

There's a thud on the floor in the entrance hall.

The noise came from a pillar.

Pablo is lying there as if he's dead.

Michelangelo's Masterpiece

As you examine Pablo, you can detect his breathing. It's fast and shallow, but he's alive. There's hope for him yet!

Could the poison in the sealing wax be to blame?

"Some fiendish potion masters were at work five hundred years ago."

Mr. Tonatelli has tears in his eyes. *"I have heard of poisons whose effects come and go, as with Pablo. But then at some point..."*

He presses his lips together, unwilling and unable to continue.

After sniffing hard, he says in a strangled voice, *"Come on. You must go back to see Michelangelo again."*

You were really close to him before, only he couldn't see you.

"This time it will be different," Mr. Tonatelli insists. He carries the unconscious dog in his arms like a sleeping baby and keeps rubbing his cheek against Pablo's cold nose. He leads you up to the second floor.

A massive picture frame hangs in a deep, wide alcove. It's at least twice the size of a large door, and it's most unusual in every respect.

The frame ticks. It consists of clocks of every conceivable size, all ticking. Each one shows a different time, and the hands of some are racing around at high speed.

Inside its frame the picture is just black—not a flat black surface, but a swirling black mist.

Side by side in the center of the lower edge of the frame are four white enameled dials.

"This is the Picture of Time. Set the hands."

Mr. Tonatelli gives you the times you are to enter.

They are all full hours. *"This must be the right year,"* he says finally, satisfied.

The black mist dissolves like clouds when the sun breaks through.

But it's not the sun that appears, it's a part of a painting.

The picture moves slowly, as if you're viewing it through a video camera, and the scene changes. You hear choral singing in the distance—the sort of chanting without words that is normally only heard in churches. This painting seems to be made up of many parts—another piece has already appeared from below—and each picture tells a story.

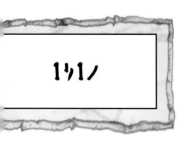

Which year has been entered?

A respectful silence has fallen. Mr. Tonatelli lovingly strokes Pablo's head. *"Michelangelo's masterpiece,"* he whispers.

But Michelangelo was a sculptor. And perhaps something of an architect, as he designed the chapel you visited earlier.

"It's hard to believe, but Michelangelo didn't want to accept this commission at first. He always regarded himself as a sculptor. What he has created here are painted figures that look like statues. This is a fresco—a wall painting. The colors are applied directly to the damp plaster, and they bond with it. They glow like windows into other worlds, don't they?"

More and more images appear in the frame.

"The pope imagined only the twelve apostles on the ceiling of the Sistine Chapel in Rome," Mr. Tonatelli continues, *"But Michelangelo created this magnificent work."*

92

" It's the size of a tennis court. He painted three hundred figures."

The woman in the image that comes into view next looks like a man. While the scene floats sideways across the frame you get a chance to see the reddish strokes of Michelangelo's sketches. He actually seems to have drawn the body of a man. Mr. Tonatelli can explain.

"The male body was idolized five hundred years ago. It says in the Bible that God created man and then took one of his ribs to make woman. Therefore, artists particularly liked to portray male bodies."

/(ˉ_ɜϽ(ɜ~ˉ

You only have one seal left to open.
The drawing on the parchment may have
something to do with this gigantic painting. What stories do the
paintings tell? Aren't they stories from the Bible?

The complete
fresco is shown at the
back

What story does this
part of the fresco tell?

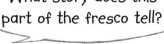

IHI CI IAIICII

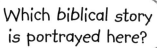

God is giving
life to this man.
Who is he?

ΛΙΛΓ Ι

Which biblical story
is portrayed here?

IHI SICI /CI HCAII'S AII

"*Michelangelo painted for four years. At first he was doubtful he could finish the commission and wanted another artist to take over!*" Mr. Tonatelli continues. "*He had already painted a large area when part of the fresco went moldy during an icy winter. Nevertheless, Michelangelo finished the ceiling.*" Now the whole chapel is visible. Part of it is filled by scaffolding.

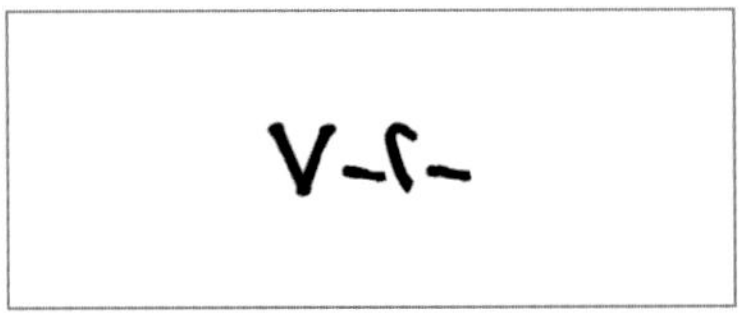

V–ſ–

"*It's twice as high as the highest diving board at the swimming pool! Over eighty feet!*" Mr. Tonatelli tells you. Michelangelo stands painting right at the top. His head is tilted back and he can only see a small part of the picture above him. Assistants work alongside him. They are holding a large piece of paper up against the ceiling. You can see a sketch on it. Lots of tiny holes have been punched along the lines. The assistants are rubbing coal dust over the paper so that little black dots are left on the plaster when they take it away.

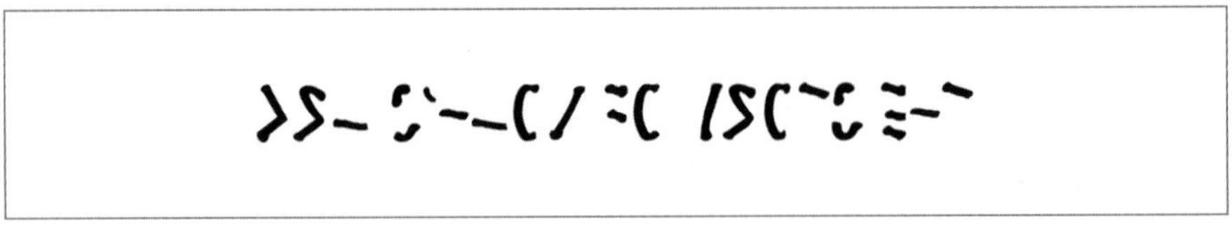

)S– ;–-(/ ꝛC /SꞆ-ꞓ ꞓ–

"Master Michelangelo!" Mr. Tonatelli calls.

"Don't disturb me. I must get this finished. The pope is already getting impatient." Michelangelo has splashes of paint in his beard.

"People say that after Michelangelo had finished, he could only read letters if he held them up above his head," Mr. Tonatelli tells you under his breath.

An assistant brings a bowl of mixed paint.

"Master, you've completed that big picture above you in just one day," he marvels.

But Michelangelo doesn't appear to have heard him.

The brush scratches over the damp plaster, and when the pig's bristles get stuck in it, Michelangelo doesn't even bother to pull them out.

NOW YOU CAN OPEN THE FINAL SEAL, NO. 7.

Mr. Tonatelli tries again. *"Master Michelangelo, the secret chamber with the seven seals."*

Michelangelo stops painting and leans forward. He stretches his back, which must be incredibly painful.

How can he hear Mr. Tonatelli? Is he able to see you?

"It is said that a dark secret is hidden there. Some of the seals are

poisoned," Mr. Tonatelli says, trying to draw some useful information out of Michelangelo.

Michelangelo mutters sullenly, *"Bramante! You'll get what you deserve on Judgment Day."*

"Quick!" Mr. Tonatelli points at the dials. *"Reset them."* He names the year: 1541.

The Last Judgment

Pablo gulps and opens his eyes. Puzzled, he looks at his master's face and licks him on the chin.

"Are you okay now, little one?" Mr. Tonatelli cuddles the dog and strokes him affectionately. Pablo doesn't have a clue what's going on, and frowns.

A new picture has appeared in the frame. What chaos!

"The Last Judgment. The largest fresco ever painted," Mr. Tonatelli announces, sounding like a market trader advertising his wares. Of course, it's much smaller in the picture frame, but no less impressive. So that's how Michelangelo imagined the Last Judgment.

Those who had led good lives were allowed to enter heaven, but the others were condemned to purgatory and hell. Mr. Tonatelli points to a figure holding something in his hand that looks like a rubber mask.

"Saint Bartholomew—his skin was flayed," Mr. Tonatelli explains. *"Look closely. Does the face look familiar? Michelangelo painted this*

fresco behind the altar of the Sistine Chapel. At the time, many people complained about the nudity of the figures. After Michelangelo's death, one of his students was commissioned by the pope to paint draperies over them."

Mr. Tonatelli puts his struggling dog down and straightens up with a groan. But this time it's not caused by the pain in his back.

"Last Judgment." Annoyed with himself, he shakes his head.

Whose face is that?

"Michelangelo meant the Last Judgment, when evildoers would be punished."

The hooded man! He is the key. He must know. Wasn't he at the quarry in Carrara? Donatella saw him there.

"Listen!" Mr. Tonatelli leans his heavy arm on your shoulders. *"Downstairs is the piece of marble you brought back. Very clever of you. It will help you to get back to Carrara through the hole under the pillar. While you're falling, think about this hooded man. See him in your mind's eye. Visualize every tiny detail. It's important. The power of your mind can take you back to the moment when the hooded man was seen in the quarry."*

That doesn't sound so difficult. Or does it? What did the hooded man look like? Exactly? Take a close look at his feet.

"Pablo's going to stay here. This time you'll have to manage without him. He's too weak!" Mr. Tonatelli says, holding the dog tightly by the collar. What a shame. He's such a good companion.

Pablo whimpers sadly.

> What did the hooded man look like? Look at his feet. Here's a tip: compare them with page 37!

Ɔↄ.ƷƐ/⌐.Ʒ⊰ V

What Is in the Secret Chamber?

Donatella runs up to you, waving both hands. She recognizes you again immediately. She obviously hasn't spent so much time in the quarry today. Her jacket is still ruby red and her frayed pants are olive green.

"I saw him!" she reports, wide-eyed.

"*He came with three other men, dressed in black. They were all scowling.*"

Donatella screws up her rosy face. "*Come with me!*"

Donatella leads you to the edge of the rock. A steep slope falls away almost vertically below you. Lying on your stomach, you peer over the edge.

There are two carriages parked at the foot of the mountain. The horses are drinking thirstily from a leather bucket the driver is holding. It is just as Donatella described. Four men are staring up at the quarry, but the hooded man is not among them. What did Donatella tell you earlier?

"*He's not wearing his habit this time,*" she says, as if it were the most obvious thing in the world. So that's what the hooded man looks like without his cowl! Their voices carry up the mountain to where you are lying. You are able to eavesdrop on their conversation.

"It should be here, Your Honor. And inside you'll find proof that

Which of the four men is the hooded man?

Michelangelo is in league with the devil. That's why he must never be involved in building the cathedral. Lucifer himself painted the frescos in the chapel on his behalf."

The men look doubtful. One purses his lips and says, "What's this secret supposed to be? And what's the proof?"

"Michelangelo is creating living statues in that chamber. He's carving warriors. Although he's older than any of us, he hacks into the stone more fiercely than three young stonemasons."

Another of the men speaks up. "Do you think he's planning to launch these stone warriors against our dukes?"

"And against the pope!" The hooded man expels the words like a shot.

"I know the chamber," Donatella whispers to you, and jumps up. Like a mountain goat, she scrambles over the fallen boulders, runs along a narrow path, fights her way through the undergrowth, pulls aside long branches with dried-out leaves and finally points proudly at a gray marble door. It's not made from a single piece, but from many chunks skillfully stacked one on top of the other. Something strikes you immediately. Some of the stones bear the symbols that you saw beneath the seals.

LAY A PIECE OF PAPER ON TOP OF THE SECRET STONE DOOR
AND TRACE OR PAINT OVER THE SHAPES THAT
ARE MARKED WITH A SYMBOL THAT YOU RECOGNIZE.

Like a Golden Sky

What's that about? What does Michelangelo mean by that? Donatella points to herself and says *"Io! That means 'I' in Italian."*

Their legs white with marble dust, the powerful men now reach the entrance too. You and Donatella lie hidden behind a bush.

The hooded man explains self-importantly, *"Don't be afraid of the poison in the seals. I've found out what it is. Michelangelo has used the juice of a purple berry that makes people unconscious. These herbs are the antidote. All you need to do is drink a tea made from this mixture."* He holds up a small pouch that's dangling from his belt. *"Then you'll be fine again."*

You can find the secret stone door on the back cover of the book.

The man he addressed as 'Your Honor', who must be a judge, examines the stacked boulders.

"Have them removed," he orders.

"I must warn you, what you will find in there could make you blind, or even kill you!"

The hooded man holds up his hands, trying to put the men off.

Now the third man butts in, "You're one of those jealous people who want to cause trouble for Michelangelo."

"Are you trying to insult me, sir?" the hooded man says, pretending to take offense.

As proof of his innocence, he turns toward the stones and pulls a piece of parchment from his jacket. There are symbols scribbled on it—the same as those beneath the seals. When the hooded man grabs the stone marked with a circle and a dot, the whole entrance begins to wobble. The chunks of marble tremble. Sand and splinters trickle down. The hooded man quickly jumps backward, out of harm's way.

"Do you need further evidence?" he shrieks.

"*You have produced evidence of your own evil intrigue!*" a gruff voice growls.

"Master Michelangelo!" The judge bows his head respectfully. Michelangelo has appeared in the clearing, accompanied by two stonemasons.

"*I may look like a scarecrow. My teeth chatter, and I have a cricket chirping in one ear and a spider's web in the other!*"

The serious men can't suppress a smile when they hear him describe himself like this. *"However, I'm not in league with evildoers."* Groveling, the hooded man excuses himself.

"I'll show you the secret hidden in the chamber I've created here. I have been protecting it from my enemies. It's something I haven't been able to stop thinking about for a long time. Only I can open the door."

Donatella digs you in the ribs. It's all clear now. "I" is IO, and a key is not necessary. You just need to move a single stone. Michelangelo asks the men to step back and turns toward the door he has constructed.

> Which *stone* is that?

Thanks to his work as a sculptor, Michelangelo is very strong, even in his old age. He pulls the stone out as if it were made of cardboard. There's no rumbling or wobbling. This time the door doesn't threaten to collapse. The stonemasons take away three large boulders to create a narrow gap. The men squeeze through it, followed by Michelangelo. The hooded man slips away unnoticed. His evil plan has been foiled. He didn't succeed in doing Michelangelo any harm. He wasn't able to prevent him from working on St. Peter's Cathedral.

The pouch! When the hooded man slinks past, grab it from his belt.
He won't protest.

Minutes elapse.

When the men come out of the cave, they find it difficult to speak.
You can see from their faces how incredible they found what they have
just seen.

*"That's how I imagine it. That's how it should look. And I don't
expect to be paid for it,"* Michelangelo explains.

The judge bows deeply. "Only you, great master, only you can construct
it. So it shall be. I myself will see to it."

Michelangelo accompanies the men back to their carriages. You and
Donatella finally have a chance to take a look in the cave.

CRISCC/I E/C^S E^
^FIS SC^ .CI

Although there's hardly any light coming in from the entrance, it's
bright inside. Warm, golden light surrounds you.

"How on earth...?" Donatella gasps, filled with awe.

The walls of the cave are slightly sloping, only roughly finished, and
uneven, with many dark veins running through them.

Michelangelo has carved a cupola in the roof of the cave. It arches
above you like a protective tent. Sunlight streams in from the top and
bathes the cupola in golden light.

Angels and saints gaze down benignly.

"Do you feel it? Do you feel how they are watching over us?" Donatella whispers.

You sense a feeling of security, of calm and of peace. Time seems to be standing still, and when you tilt your head back, it feels as if you're being pulled upward by unseen hands.

It's not easy to tear yourself away from this sight, but Pablo is waiting for you in the museum, and he needs those herbs urgently.

Donatella gives you a little marble ball as a parting gift.

Later you are standing with Mr. Tonatelli looking at the book about Michelangelo. He has opened it at a page that shows the amazing cupola.

"It's the cupola of St. Peter's in Rome," he explains. *"Michelangelo was actually allowed to build it according to his plans. You must go to Rome one day and see it for yourself. It's a hundred times bigger than the first model in the cave."*

Pablo has greedily slurped up the herb tea—not a drop was left in his bowl. Now he's not only cured of the effects of the poison, he has even more energy than before.

The storm has passed. Mr. Tonatelli asks you to take Pablo out for a quick walk. He's still finding it difficult to walk himself.

"You must come back and visit us," he insists.

Pablo barks enthusiastically.

"We would be very pleased to see you again soon."

Mr. Tonatelli looks longingly at the little marble ball in your hand.
He points at it hesitantly.
"Could you possibly leave that here with me? I would love to put it on display."
He tells you about Leonardo da Vinci's paintbrush and
Vincent van Gogh's palette, which now belong to him.

Do you know where the paintbrush and palette came from? If not, it's time for another adventure to "Crack the Leonardo da Vinci Code" or "Save Vincent's Hidden Treasure."

Somewhere in the museum a door squeaks. Behind it another adventure is already beginning…

Hello!

People often ask me if the Museum of Adventures actually exists. Well, yes and no! The idea came to me when I visited a small museum and the electricity was cut off. I found myself alone in the dark rooms and felt as if I was lost in a maze. That's when the idea for the Museum of Adventures came to me!

By the way, I've already started work on the next adventure…

See you soon, *Thomas Brezina*

Thomas Brezina's books have turned millions of children into keen readers and he has been called "the Pied Piper of reading". His successful thrillers and adventure series for boys and girls have been translated into over thirty languages. In China, where his books have topped the bestseller lists for years, he is known as the "master of adventures."

His lively style enthralls his young readers, who feel as if he's sitting beside them, telling the story. "I only write a sentence if I think that it will bring a sparkle to my readers' eyes," he says.

Laurence Sartin

has brought clever little Pablo—and much more—to life in this book.

He has illustrated numerous books for children and young adults and lives in France and Germany, where he teaches design and illustration at the Akademie Regensburg.

The works in this book

The images of Michelangelo's works are taken from *Ich, Michelangelo*, Prestel, Munich, Berlin, London, New York, 2003.

Thomas Brezina
"Who Can Crack the
Leonardo da Vinci Code?"
112 pages with numerous
illustrations and interactive
elements: puzzle booklet,
foil mirror and ancient
treasury scroll
Paperback with flaps
7¾ x 9½ in. / 19.5 x 24 cm
ISBN 3-7913-3322-4

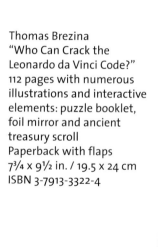

Thomas Brezina
"Who Can Save Vincent's Hidden
Treasure?"
96 pages with numerous
illustrations and interactive
elements: decoder, letters and
treasure map
Paperback with flaps
7¾ x 9½ in. / 19.5 x 24 cm
ISBN 3-7913-3432-8

The Library of Congress Cataloguing-in-Publication data is available;
British Library Cataloguing-in-Publication Data:
a catalogue record for this book is available
from the British Library; Deutsche Bibliothek
holds a record of this publication in the
Deutsche Nationalbibliografie;
detailed bibliographical data can be found under: http://dnb.ddb.de

Prestel books are available worldwide. Please contact
your nearest bookseller or one of the addresses below
for information concerning your local distributor.

The title of the "Museum of Adventures" series is protected by copyright.

© Prestel Verlag, Munich · Berlin · London · New York 2006

Prestel Verlag
Königinstrasse 9, 80539 Munich
Tel. +49 (89) 38 17 09-0
Fax +49 (89) 38 17 09-35

Prestel Publishing Ltd.
4, Bloomsbury Place, London WC1A 2QA
Tel. +44 (020) 7323-5004
Fax +44 (020) 7636-8004

Prestel Publishing
900 Broadway, Suite 603, New York, NY 10003
Tel. +1 (212) 995-2720; Fax +1 (212) 995-2733

www.prestel.com

Translated from the German by Pat Jacobs
Editorial direction: Katharina Haderer,
UK/US editions edited by Fawkes Publishing Limited, Twickenham
Design and layout: agenten und freunde, Munich
Origination: w&co MediaServices, Munich
Printing and Binding: Print Consult, Munich

Printed on acid-free paper

ISBN 3-7913-3556-1